Things for Black People on a whole is not very easy. Our history, and identity have, and has been masked; hidden from us. Our intellect downgraded.

We're classed lower than low yet, with all our advancements throughout the ages; blacks on a whole do not value their true identity; worth, and self worth.

Many things we created; invent, were stolen. Many could not put their names on inventions; thus others; other races stole their birthright; gold, and prosperity; right to life.

But for the few who know; knowledge is key; one of the keys to life. They know what the Black Race can, and cannot do. Yet, for many; our technological advancements must not be known. We of ourselves fail to realize that; without the Black Race, humanity would fail to exist; would not exist literally.

Cease

We are a smart race of people; thus, we are builders; the creators of it all.

Many of these books will celebrate Life; Black Life, and Black Smarts. I cannot hide who we are, and never will hide who we are.

I am "BLACK," and I am more than truly proud of my "BLACK LIFE, AND HERITAGE."

Within this book, there are no chapters. I truly cannot write chapter books in this line of books. However, a line; and or, the line you see in these and or, some of these books, are my new chapter. I've written chapter books yes, but I am not one to follow the format of any book. I write therefore, I cannot adhere to conventional writing methods literally.

So sit back and enjoy.

Know the way I write therefore, know life.
For me, life isn't the colour of your skin, and never will be; therefore, I educate you on life in the Michelle Jean series of books.

Yes, I can be racist in some of the books I write, but think beyond colour. Truly look to life.

ANYTHING FOR YOU   Snow ft. Nadine Sutherland, Beenie Man, and others.

Michelle

"Damn I'm late," realizing the time.

"Free are you okay?"

"I will be," looking at her friend as she tried to mask her concerns. She knew Dennis would be upset. He was one that did not like lateness, and with her trying to finish her studies put a damper on their relationship. Hurrying home to a furious Dennis; the yelling match began.

"Why are you late, and don't you dare tell me you were studying in the library?" Said the bulky tied-end before her. Dennis was tall with the most beautiful chocolate skin you had ever seen. His hair was cut low and wavy. He was rough with a temper to back him up.

"Dennis you know I was. I have an assignment to do for which I need to do research."

"You could have done your research here on the computer. As ot late you've been late every day from school and frankly, I'm tired of it. You're my wife, and you are to be home with dinner ready when I get home."

"Excuse me! I am not your maid. Like you, I need a career, and I will not get that sitting at home babysitting you."

"You're my wife," he yelled.

"Yes, I'm your wife,' she yelled back. 'But there is more to life than just being your wife."

"What more? You're there to serve me, and as of late you are not doing it. Therefore, you have to drop your classes."

"I refuse to drop out of school for you Dennis. This is my life, and you don't run it."

Going up to Free he grabbed her and said; "I run it, now you are quitting school."

"And I told you, I am not quitting school to please you. This is my life and I run it. I need a future outside of this home," standing her ground.

Flooring her, Free held her face. She felt the blood in her nose, and in her mouth. "Like I said; you are my wife, and you are quitting school."

Looking at Dennis with hatred she wanted to seriously hurt him, but couldn't. She could not cry. All she could do was hold her face. Dennis did not want her to have a future, but she was determined to have a future no matter the cost.

Cleaning up herself Free prepared dinner for him. She did not want any further confrontation with him. She had to hold her peace she kept telling herself in her head. She had to bare on, and bare the pain. She had to take his abuse for the time being. She knew what she had to do, and was doing it. All these things Free kept telling herself. She had to be strong, and hold on for a little while longer. She could not give up despite the pain and abuse she was facing, and enduring.

• • •

Thankful it was the weekend; she spent all weekend tending to her injuries. Not thinking of the pain she felt; her focus was on accomplishing her dream, and that was to graduate university, and have a career. She could not let Dennis stop her from achieving. He had his career. She did not hinder him yet, he was hindering her; did not want her to pursue her goal, or succeed in life.

Defying her husband she went to school that Monday. Studying she went home late, and the same thing happened. This time she did not get hit in the face, but in the stomach. Her husband was adamant in her quitting school. His aim was to see her fail, and he was going to make her fail at all cost. For him, it was either she quit her studies or, take the abuse. And he was abusing her physically, and mentally.

Fed up Free went to the door, and he pulled her back to him. "I am going to my mother's house Dennis. She has something for me."

"I will come with you."

"I do not need you following me to my mother's house. The both of you do not get along, nor does she like you. Therefore, where no bones are provided, no dogs are invited, and she's told you this categorically over and over again."

"Your mother is a bitch."

"And what is yours? Isn't she the community pipe stand?" And she felt a fist so hard she thought she was going to have a heart attack.

Catching her breath she waited for the pain to subside. Going through the door she slammed it behind her, and walked to her mother's house. Seeing her daughter Free's mother did not have a pleased look on her face. She knew the hardship Free was facing in her marriage. The abuse she was taking; the lies that were being told by him. He did not want to see her daughter succeed, and was doing all to see her fail. He was a burden to her; hence he did all to break Free down.

"When did you turn his beating stick?" Free's mother said before she could say anything.

"Mother."

"Free, you truly do not want me to get involved because if I do; he's a dead man. So I suggest you handle it before I do. I did not raise you to be any man's beating stick so whatever peace you are holding, you squash it before I ignite the war."

"He wants me to quit school."

"Quit school! Is he paying for your schooling, or are you just his beating stick? Someone he can bully. When did you get so weak, and submissive?"

"Mother"

"Don't mother me," and Free's mother got up to go to her house, and Free held her hand. She needed her mother to keep the peace, and not start a war. She knew what she was doing, and she had to let true peace reign. She could not let her mother ignite the war.

"I will handle it."

"You had better because cop, or no cop he truly do not want me to get involved. Now look on the table, your father sent you something. His sister should be down in a couple of weeks. He said she has a suitcase for you."

"Tell him thanks."

"I will. Now handle your business," her mother said sternly.

"Yes mam."

"Your room is free; waiting for you when you are ready. You are protected so I suggest you lose the loser. Divorce his ass. Oh, Braun called. His offer still stands."

"Mom, Braun and I have been over for years."

"It's business Free; so I suggest you look into things, and move on with your life."

"Is the house finished?"

"You know it's finished. You know the business is going well. You know everything."

"Yes mam."

Getting the money from off her dresser, Free left her mother's house without saying another word.

Going to school the next day she saw Deuce. Sitting beside her he said; "we have all we need, and I am sorry you had to go through the abuse."

"You owe me," looking at the handsome detective before her.

"I know, and trust me, I know he's going to pay at your hands, and the hands of others."

"Yeah. The divorce?" Asked Freedom

"Guaranteed"

"You take care," said Freedom. She was free now. Her obligation to Deuce was over. She had her life back, and she was going to live it. Deuce knew this because they were family.

"You too."

Leaving school early Free went home and packed all her things. When Dennis got home he said; "what's this?"

"I am leaving, plus I'm divorcing you." She did not have to hold the peace any longer. She wanted the war to start so she could finish it her way.

"Divorce me and leaving, you can't divorce me, or leave because I own you."

"Later Dennis."

Putting his hand on Free he said, "you can't leave."

Gently taking his hand off her, Free turned to him and said, "I am leaving, and there isn't a damned thing you can do about it." Stern in her words.

"Are you challenging me?" And she gave him no time to react. What came next rocked, and floored him. She wasn't playing anymore. It was her time, and turn to punish him for his abuse; him abusing her.

"I played your little nasty games, and I made you abuse me for far too long, now it's payback time."

Lounging at Free she connected with a right hook to the nose. Pounding his face in with her fist; it was Deuce that had to pull her off him. Leaving Dennis a bloody mess she took her bag and went to her mother's place. She had wanted to do more damage, but Deuce saved him. Every pain she felt, she wanted Dennis to feel more than two times over. She was his beating stick and punching bag, but no more. She was free, free of him and his abuse; bullshit. She had her life and freedom back, and she wasn't going to look back. Her full future was before her, and she was going to take it, and live it.

"Your dinner is on the table," her mother said with a smile on her face.

• • •

Jumping out of sleep sweating Freedom took deep breaths. "Oh God what am I doing?"

Wiping her face she called Braun. Answering sleepily he said, "Freedom are you okay?"

"No"

"Nightmare again?"

"Yes"

"Then do what is right for you. It's obvious this guy you are talking to is not the right one for you."

"Braun he seem so nice."

"Seem nice is different from what you are seeing. Now, have you considered my offer?"

"Yes, Mr. Billionaire I have, and the answer is yes. Considering he's paying for my education."

"She has a full scholarship that I managed to get transferred to one of the top universities in the country. She has absolutely nothing to worry about."

"How did I meet you again?"

"She submitted a project to my firm when she was twelve that looked promising from her concept drawing. A concept that I personally looked into, and is implementing."

"Yeah, and I thank you because he's had my back from I was a child."

"She's dear to me. A true friend, and someone I can talk to about anything regardless of our age difference. She is extremely intelligent for her age, and now at sixteen she is going to university."

"I just hope he still can protect me."

"I can and will."

"Good. Now, will you be picking me up, or do I have to take the plane by myself?"

"My assistant will be picking you up, and taking you to the university. I know you do not like taking planes, and you have never travelled out of your home country."

"Bah"

"Arc wc acting tough now?"

"Yes, but I would rather you get me."

"Young lady, have you forgotten that I am going away for three month?"

"Yes; by choice because, you know I do not forget anything."

"True, but you will be fine. Besides, I can call you undetected anytime I want to no matter where I am in the world."

"Yeah, yeah."

"You know you are making the right decision. You saw what your future would be like with this guy. You're young so truly live."

"Should I tell him I am leaving?"

"No"

"Why?"

"Your safety. You are seeing his true nature."

"And my parents."

"Can handle themselves, and you know this."

"True, but I am worried about my siblings."

"Your siblings are glad they are getting rid of you."

"True. I challenge them too much."

"That you do."

"Well I better let you get back to sleep, and I do hope you miss me a lot. Think of me."

"How can I not little lady. You drive me crazy at times."

"Hey, we are true friends that respect each other. Besides, I'm too young for you."

"That you are. Later spud."

"Later Braun."

And Braun was true to his word. His secretary did get Freedom, and bring her to the university. Staying with Freedom for a week Braun's secretary made sure she had someone to cook for her, and show her around town. She was not allowed to go anywhere by herself.

Three months into her stay at the university Braun came to visit her.

"Braun it's cold. Does it get colder than this?"

"Yes," as they walked in the cold.

Taking some of the snow Free put it on his face, and he shivered and laughed. "You are truly not used to snow."

"No, the tropics do not see snow, and I am glad."

"Come," taking her to the local coffee shop he ordered two large hot chocolates, and a slice of banana cake to eat.

"Thank you."

"You are most welcome," feeling like a little school boy.

"So my darling friend, how was your trip, and why did you not call me frequently? Why did you turn off Freelander, and who is she that captured your eye and heart? Is she pretty? Is she cute and cuddly? How tall is she? How rich is she? How intelligent is she?"

"Wow, you don't miss a thing do you?"

"I'm not done."

"Slow down little lady. When did you become so interested in my personal life?"

"He's the man of the year, and a lot of the girls at the university is smitten by you; with some wanting to lay with you on a personal level."

"And you know this because?"

"They say you are hot. Which is weird because I cannot see the heat rising from your body, hence your body temperature is normal."

"And you know this because?"

"Your heat signature has not changed. Well it did slightly when I put the snow on your face, but that was it."

"Young lady."

"Maybe one day I will teach you about heat signature of humans if he permits me."

"It is too complex for me."

"Not for me."

"I know not for you; hence you can tell when I am not feeling well."

Looking at him googly eyed she said; "well, are you going to tell me all I need to know?"

"No, Miss Nosy."

"You know I will find out."

"I know you will."

Having their hot chocolate and cake, Braun walked her back to her apartment where he spent some time with her.

"What are you creating?" Looking at her concept drawing on the computer.

"I don't know yet."

"Freedom, I know you, and what you are capable of."

"Then you know I saw you kissing her."

"You were spying on me."

"No"

"You were spying on me. How many times have I told you not to spy on me? My personal life is my personal life. Now you are invading my privacy. I have boundaries Free, and you are over stepping yours with me."

"I'm sorry Braun."

"Are you?" He snapped.

"I am, besides she's not for you anyway. Not pretty, or educated enough."

"Young lady."

"I do not approve. Now my professor is more your type."

"I bet. Some old dragon lady."

"You know the faculty here, and there are no dragon ladies on staff."

"No match making, and no more meddling in my personal life."

"You need a girlfriend that matches you."

"Little lady, privacy."

"Alright."

"Good. Now I have to go. So behave yourself."

"Whatever"

Kissing her a top her head, he was gone with a smile on his face. He knew she was not going to stop, and that made him shake his head.

Going into his office the following Monday his secretary confronted him.

"How is she doing so far?" Concerned about Freedom's studies.

"Poorly"

"Poorly," surprised that Freedom was not performing to expectations.

"Academically, she's superior to her classmates; people wise, she is doing poorly. According to her professors she is not challenged. Her work is done way before the due date, she whizzes through her tests where others are challenged. She's gifted, and smarter than all."

"What should I do?" Still concerned about Freedom's studies.

"Bring her here. She's finished her studies already."

"What?" Surprised that Freedom would be finished her studies already.

"Her professors have not seen anyone like her. She makes them look stupid."

"Damn," wiping his face. He knew she was a prodigy but to surpass the geniuses in her classes he was not expecting. He thought she would be challenged but now he knew he was wrong.

"Braun, Dr. Daniels need help with his concept. Let her help him."

"You know he would not go for that."

"No he won't, but you are the owner of this company. She can further his research."

"You know the man, and how he likes to work alone."

"Yes I do, but what he is working on could revolutionize medicine."

"I know, but to throw Freedom into the mix just like that; is insane."

"What do you have to lose?"

"Billions"

"Are you so sure? She's not challenged. Dr. Daniels have not made any head way with his concept, maybe Freedom can help him."

"I'll think about it, and talk to Dr. Daniels."

"I'll talk to him."

"You do that." He still could not come to terms with Free finishing her studies already.

Sitting by herself, someone sat at the table beside her.

"You know you don't belong here." Looking at Free with jealousy, and distaste.

He knew her smarts, and was not pleased that Free was smarter than him. He was way older than her, and used to be the smartest one on campus. Now here she was getting all the credit, and whizzing through her work without being challenged.

What she knew; none knew. Not even their professors knew.

"Why because someone is smarter than you, and you are not getting all the accolades anymore?

"This is my school," he snapped and shouted.

"I do not see your name on it."

"You think you're smart."

"Smarter than you for you to be sitting here, and talking to me about trivial matters due to jealousy."

"Like I said, you don't belong here."

"And your petty treats truly do not scare me. So I would watch my back if I were you."

"Are you threatening me?"

"I don't have to. And to be honest with you, I truly do not care, or give a damn who your family knows on the board of directors. You finally have some competition, and you can't handle it."

"Nig," and he caught himself.

"Say it, niggers aren't supposed to be smart. They're to be in the fields picking cotton for your ancestors."

"And why the hell not? You people don't know business, or how to run the world. We do hence, you have your place on the back of the bus where ya'll belong." Mocking Freedom.

"Yet, many inventions of Blacks in the past your ancestors stole, and put their name on it because they weren't smart enough to invent them. Yes, we are at the back of the bus relaxed and happy. We will always stay back because we see and know, hence your societies are crap, filled with hate, and shit. What we can fix you cannot. What we can invent, and do invent you cannot. Therefore, slow and steady we go just waiting for your race to run everything amok like you always do, but this time around, we will not clean up after you, or clean up your mess. Duly remember the traffic lights, modern day advancement in medicine, the pyramids, ancient civilization, delicate eye operations, the laser that we invented long before your so-called history, mathematics that your ancestors stole, this earth that we designed and created; gave birth to. I am a living testament that we are smarter, and you feel threatened by me. I show you up stupid. Now get the hell away from me."

"I will make you regret coming here."

"I already regret coming here you racist, jealous, insecure, and petty child."

"This isn't over peasant."

"Peasant. I suggest you check your family's bank account combined compared to mine as it's obvious, you don't know what peasant is."

Furious he left, and Freedom smiled.

Finding his friends they asked; "well how did it go?"

"It didn't, but my father will hear about this, and we will get her out. Her sorts we truly do not need here."

Getting Freedom from school Braun did not have a pleased look on his face. The phone call he got was not pleasing.

"I know you better than that Braun, so truly do not save face with me. I know you got a call that was not pleasing to you, so truly do not hide anything from me." Freedom said before Braun could say anything.

"You were racist," he snapped.

"How was I racist?" She snapped back.

Catching himself Braun said; "I won't even bother because I know you too well when it comes to defending you and your smarts, your culture, your people, your true history, me, and others. No doubt someone feels threatened that you are smarter than them."

"Then why are we having this conversation?"

"Little lady."

"Take me to dinner."

"No"

"Why?"

"You are a child. I do not do dinner with children."

"Liar. Now take me to dinner."

"Right now?" He said like a child. She was his best friend, and although she was sixteen, he could not resist her charm. He was twenty eight years old, and knew all about her, and her inventions. Inventions that kept his company at number one due to her smarts. She secured his future financially, and he hers.

"Yes"

"Freedom,' stopping himself he said, 'alright."

Taking her to his favorite restaurant all eyes was on them when their waiter brought them to their table.

"Why is everyone staring at us?"

"I am with a very gorgeous young lady."

• • •

"Why thank you." Helping her to sit down, she took off her back pack, and he put it beside him. Leaving them a menu, the waiter was gone.

"Have all your gadgets inside?"

"Yes"

"So young lady; why did you want me to take you to dinner?"

"I'm bored, and I am not challenged."

"You want a challenge?" Braun smiled and asked.

"Yes," looking at him innocently.

"Do not look at me with those innocent eyes young lady. I know you all too well."

"Do you now?"

"I do. You have this irresistible charm about you."

Returning the waiter asked if they were ready to order.

"We have not looked at the menu as yet, can you give us some time?" Said Braun

"That won't be necessary, I know what I want." Said Freedom

"Then be my guest," smiling at Free. with amazement.
She was young yet so brilliant for her age.

She never ceased to amaze him, and he was amazed at her. She was sixteen and wealthier than most. Her intelligence none could surpass, and he knew this first hand.

"I would like your garden salad to start with. No dressing, two rolls, and for my main course, I would like to have your chicken alfredo with cucumbers, and tomatoes sliced on the side. To drink; I would like a sprite with a twist of lime in the glass, and a twist of lime on the side with a straw. For the gentleman, he would have; white wine, steak well done, your soup of the day, with one roll, and that would be all thank you."

"You ordered perfectly."

"Thank you," and the waiter was gone with a smile on his face.

"Do remind me to take all your gadgets from you."

"You can, but I would just recreate them again."

"Since you are not challenged, I have a challenge for you."

"Oh God not working with Dr. Daniels on his project that he can't seem to get ahead on."

"Yes, working with Dr. Daniels."

"Trust, I do not trust him, and you know that. Nor do I trust your secretary slash assistant."

"Do you trust anyone?"

"Aside from you, my family, and my creations, no."

"Okay, then build me a rocket ship."

"I would, but you do not have the facility for it, so I can't."

"Impossible"

"How am I impossible, unless you do not trust me?"

"Bite your tongue young lady." He trusted her wholeheartedly. She was his best friend and confidant. Nothing he hid from her. Not that he could. Despite her age, she was his life, and saving grace.

She built him, and he built her in all she did in life.

"It would hurt, so I cannot bite it. Thank you." As the waiter put their appetizer's down.

Hearing the beeping sound in her back she said; "pass my bag please."

And Braun did. Taking out a modified version of a tablet she put it to stand, and looked at the screen. "You modified a tablet to have a stand that comes out automatically, and turns on automatically?"

"Yes, or you can touch the screen without swiping it for it to come on. It's all up to you."

"And the range?"

"Global, and farther."

"Please tell me it uses satellite."

"Satellites are outdated you know that."

"Not for billions of people."

"Hence, I am alone in the world with my technological advancements. You know what I can do with technology. Therefore, the sun and moon is a clean and reliable energy source for those who know how to harvest, and harness this energy source."

"I know this Freedom."

"Then stick with me."

"How can I not Now is that a live feed of the outside of your apartment?"

"Yes"

"They are wearing masks."

"That's very observant of you Sherlock."

"Stop with the sarcasm Free because this is serious. Someone is trying to hurt you," he said sternly as he was concerned for her safety.

"Sherlock"

"Free stop, I said this is serious."

"I know Braun."

"I'm calling the police."

"Braun I have my own way of handling this."

"Do you now?"

"Braun just let it go."

"No, I will not let this go. I will not let anyone hurt you." He harshly and loudly say, and everyone stared at him.

"I'm a threat to a lot of the kids on campus you know that. Jealousy can, and do cause others to hurt you."

"Free you are important to me."

"I know, and I don't want you to lose any of your friends therefore, let it go."

"I truly do not care if I lose my friends. I have my true, and best friend with me. I have an entire global army of nerds that the governments know nothing about behind me. People you know. People that truly support you and your work, so shut them down if you know how to."

Smiling at Braun she said, "this is new technology that the government will want. It's patented to your company."

"You patented technology to my company without me knowing about this."

"You were too busy, so your sister and I did."

"Say no more. The both of you are like two peas in a pod, and it makes no sense for me to get upset at you. She would only get mom and dad involved, and you know I cannot win with either of them on her side, and yours."

"That's your sister calling you because she's seeing what is happening."

"Sis"

"Braun this is serious."

"I know."

"What are they putting under your door in that envelope?"

"Something to seriously hurt me."

"Dear God. How did you do that? I can see their faces inside the mask."

"So can everyone. The police should be there right about now."

"Hold it right there."

"You need to get her out of there Braun."

"I know. She can stay with me."

"No, no, no. You are too messy."

"You have no say Free," stern in his voice.

"I have a say. I am sixteen years old, I can pay for my own rent, and do things on my own."

"You can't even travel on your own because you do not like conventional travel."

"And you refuse to let me get a private plane that I can modify to suit my needs."

"You're too young."

"Braun"

"No"

"See what I mean." And Braun's sister smiled at her.

"Children we will talk because I have some splaining to do." Braun sister said comical.

"Do you want to continue with dinner?" Seeing the worried look on Free's face. He knew she was trying to act tough. She was scared for her life.

"No, I just want to go home," holding back the tears.

She knew who the culprit was. She saw him earlier. He did not want her in the school. Now this first attempt on her life due to her smarts, and their jealousy; she being smarter than them combined.

"Free"

"I want my mom and dad," and the tears came rolling down her cheeks, and she wiped them away quickly. Paying for their meal, and leaving a sizeable tip for the waiter, Freedom gathered her things and left with Braun. Taking her to his home he held her tight and said, "everything is going to be okay. I am here for you, and will always be there for you."

"Thank you," but that still did not make her feel any better. She wanted to be in the arms of her mother.

"Do you still want to go home?"

"Yes," pulling away from Braun. Going to her room she closed the door behind her, and called her mom.

"Baby are you okay?"

"Mom I'm scared."

"I know you are, but you knew this day would come where people would be jealous of you, and want to hurt you because you are smarter than them."

"But why mom, they are smart too?"

"Are they? Baby people do things to hurt others each and every day."

• • •

30

"But why mom?"

"Different reasons like; control, jealousy as you've noted, feeling superior to others. Some don't want, or need you to be smarter than them. It's especially nerve racking for some to see smart, and intelligent black people; especially, a smart young black female genius that is capable of so much."

"Mom"

"Baby be proud of you. Yes the world do not know what you are capable of. Braun knows, your true friends know. So keep those that are dear to you truly dear; close. What you can accomplish in one day, it takes many years; if not decades of research to accomplish, and even with their accomplishments, they have flaws. You've graduated from the highest university that man knows nothing about apart from a select few. You surpass all the geniuses of the world because you've found flaws in their theories therefore, you do not need their universities, nor will they be able to accommodate you intellectually. Three months, and you're graduating. You make their professors look stupid."

"Yes, but I am not challenged mom."

"Then challenge yourself. Create like you always do."

"Thanks mom," giving her a faint smile.

"And go talk to Braun. I know you locked him out because you are in your room talking to me."

• • •

"I like talking to you especially when I need a hug,"

"Hugs; did someone say hugs?"

"Nana"

"I will always truly love you, now go talk to Braun, and hug Nana. She always get in the way of our hugs."

"Yeah, later mom."

"Hugs," and Nana outstretched her arms, and Freedom kissed her and said; "I truly love you too."

Finding Braun a short time later, she went into his arms and hugged him real tight. "I am sorry for shutting you out, but I needed my mom."

"Free I am here for you. You're young, and I know you need your parents, but you have me, and my family."

"I know but I miss my family."

"Then whenever you need to go see them, I will take you."

"Right now?"

"On Friday. But we must be back by Sunday evening the latest young lady."

"Yes sir, and thank you so much. You won't regret this." Looking up at him with her baby brown eyes that was filled with tears.

"There we go again with that innocent baby look. Now you have tears in your eyes."

"I am happy, and I'd better be your baby."

"Go, go to bed young lady because tomorrow you are coming with me to work."

"Yea," and she scurried off to bed.

"She grows on you doesn't she." He heard Free's mom say from the monitor.

"Mom"

"Keep protecting her."

"Yes mam," and she was gone.

Going into work and before he could get to his office Braun's sister was pulling him, and Freedom into her office.

"The government want the technology to whatever Freedom was using to see the faces of the men in the mask."

"Why?"

"Catching thieves, bad guys. Sweetie you create technology that is unthinkable for some."

"Then you know how I feel about the government having anything of mine."

● ● ●

"I do."

"Good." Freedom did not like governments. She blamed them for a lot of the issues plaguing earth. They had no control, or say when it came to protecting the environment from greedy corporations globally. Corporations that dumped chemicals in the earth's water supply, run oil rigs a wreck so that oil could be spilled in the waterways thus; further destroying the environment. All contributed to the decay of earth then squabble about the issues facing humanity, and earth herself. They did not see them as the issue. None truly cared about protecting the environment – reversing climate change, cleaning the ocean and seas. They could not see the fundamental right of earth to live clean, and pollution free.

No government regulated the different global corporations as to the amount of feces, chemicals, human garbage dumped into the waterways of life. Therefore, Free wanted nothing to do with them, and she had nothing to do with them.

Hearing the knock at her door Braun's sister said, "come in."

"Good morning everyone. Freedom how are you this fine morning?"

"I'm fine." She did not like Braun's secretary, and Braun knew this.

"Did Braun tell you he wanted you to work with Dr. Daniels?"

"Yes, and I am sure Dr. Daniels is not pleased about this."

"No, he is not, but I am sure he will get used to it."

"Yeah" *doubted her words. Dr. Daniels was a man that did things his way. He did*

"Don't worry, all will be fine." *not share his work with anyone. He capitalized*

"Yeah," not sure of what she was getting into. *often... Free did not trust him.*

"Trust me they will be. Now if you are ready, let me introduce you to Dr. Daniels." And Freedom looked to Braun for security and he said; "all will be fine. Besides, I am taking you to lunch today considering she did not have breakfast, or dinner yesterday."

But there was no surety in her look, and Braun's sister hugged her and said in her ear; "I am there for you. Do not worry because I will not let anyone hurt you, you have my word on that."

"Okay." Lighting up she was gone with Braun's assistant.

"Are you sure this is a wise move on your part big brother?"

"No, because she does not trust either of them." Concerned for Freedom's safety. *and her work.*

"She has good reason to. They've capitalized off her earlier inventions. Work she did that they took credit for."

"Sis"

"She trusts you wholeheartedly Braun. Do not lose sight of that. Her truth is worth more than our billions, and you know this."

"I do."

"Then let Nana be around her more."

"No"

"Nana is a robot, That is her best friend as well. So you cannot isolate her Braun."

"I don't want her to create artificial intelligence sis," he said sternly.

"You cannot stop her because she has already."

"That I've asked her to destroy, and she has right sis?" Doubting his sister with that question.

"She has, and you know she has because you were right there with her. Plus, I gave you my word that all has been destroyed and it has, but it does not mean she cannot start all over again."

"I know that, and some has followed in her footsteps, but at what cost to the human race sis? You know some want total control, and once they get this, they feel they will become as God."

"And you've kept her from these people. With what happened, I know she's scared because this was the first attempt on her life."

"Because she's a threat to some. What she create, and invent; none can."

"Yes, but we have safety nets in place for her. You know the guild will, and do protect her at all cost."

"Yes, but she doesn't trust him, or her. I don't want them to influence her negatively."

"Then keep Nana around her twenty-four seven."

"Yeah"

"You cannot be jealous of Nana because she sees what you cannot. She is well designed and capable of protecting her."

"I know." *still jealous of the relationship Free had with Nana.*

"Then let her do what she was built to do without interference from you."

"Yeah." He knew the relationship Freedom had with Nana.

Nana was a mother to Freedom.

She was also Freedom's best friend. Free trusted Nana with more than her life, and he was a bit jealous even though he had a superb relationship with Free.

Finding the doctor, Freedom did not feel secure. She did not trust him. Nor, did she want to help him, or work with him. He was a wolf in sheep's clothing, and Free knew this.

"Dr. Daniels, a minute please."

"Ms. Carter, you know better than to interrupt me."

"I know, but we spoke yesterday in regards to taking on an understudy."

"And she is the understudy? She doesn't look smart."

"Trust me she is that smart."

"Freedom meet Dr. Daniels."

"I know who he is. Brilliant scientist that is trying to create new life in a completely man-made environment."

"For which many have called me mad."

"Are you not mad? Can you have a man-made environment without having the components, and the environment to keep it going?"

"You see you can, we can make a better environment without all the pitfalls of this earth."

"For which is a challenge doctor. Can man make dirt from scratch doctor? How do you equate for this new environment's heating and cooling system without

• • •

knowing how to create a new sun and moon; heating and cooling system doctor?"

Smiling Ms. Carter said; "I will leave you too alone," and she left the room.

"What do you know about particles, and wave particles. How they interact with each other?"

"In regards to what doctor; energy, speed, vibration, time, matter, solids?" And Dr. Daniels looked at her odd. No one had ever asked that question before; thus, he had to wonder just how brilliant she was? But then, she had to be that brilliant for Braun to want her to work with him he thought to himself.

Spending the morning with Dr. Daniels, she was glad when Nana came to get her.

"Is this your creation?"

"Yes"

"She does not look human like for someone of your intelligence."

"Touché doctor." As if saying, if you only knew what I can, and cannot do with artificial intelligence, and the future of technology. All the design flaws many had to give robots human features she had no problem in doing. She could design artificial intelligence to look like any human, and she has. Creations she had to destroy because Braun asked her to. They were too life like. So life like you could not tell they were robots.

Taking Nana's hand she said, "later doc," and Freedom was gone.

"Trust"

"I know baby, neither do I."

Going back to Braun's office with her holding Nana's hand, lunch was waiting for her.

"Thank you my friend, it's beautiful."

"I thought you would like it. I made lunch you know."

"I know, and I thank you so much," kissing Nana on the cheek.

"I need you to be safe and comfortable at all times therefore, Nana will be with you always when I am not there."

"So you are going away again."

"Yes, but I have to take you to see your parents first."

"Braun"

"You are safe. You will be with Nana at my home. You created a fortress there therefore, you will be safe from harm. And while I am away, no using the hover car. God forbid people knowing you designed a car that do not use conventional batteries and engines. Cars that are reliant on the sun during the day, and moon at night."

● ● ●

"You know there are other means to travel faster than the speed of light without using mechanics; machines."

"I know you know of this speed Free. So, while I am away; behave. I'm trusting you to be normal for a change."

"I cannot. I can only be me."

"Impossible. And don't elaborate further. Now, come have lunch because I know you are hungry."

Helping her to sit, Nana served them both. This was their time together before he left, and by Friday evening he was taking her with Nana to see her parents. Hugging her mother Free did not want to let her go.

"You're safe so no more worries."

"Did he come by to see why I left?"

"No. I think he knew you knew he was a rouge; someone that cannot be trusted."

"I kept dreaming about what my life would be like with him you know, and that scared me."

"I know."

"Mom, will I find the right one eventually; I mean when I grow up?"

"You are grown up beyond your years, and I am truly proud of you. And yes, you will find the right someone."

● ● ●

"Thanks mom."

Sitting with her mother they talked for a while before she had something to eat. Waking early the next morning she was with Nana in the kitchen making breakfast for everyone.

"Mom, where's my annoying siblings?"

"At your nan's with your dad. This was our time together."

"Why? I wanted and needed to see them."

"Baby it's too dangerous, and you know that. Now sit with me and have breakfast."

"Braun," looking at Braun for reassurance. He knew the danger to her family. She was smart beyond her years and many knew this. In all he did, he had to make sure Free and her family were safe all the time no matter the cost.

"Everything will be fine. Your mother is correct. It was too dangerous for them, plus the house is being watched."

Having breakfast with her mother and staying until late Sunday, Braun, Freedom, and Nana was off without incident. Going back to Braun's house she called her mother to let her know she arrived home safe, and everything was fine.

"Mom; why did dad sell the house?"

● ● ●

"Space, and he was growing tired of it. Your Nan's house suited us better, so we are expanding on it."

"And granddad is okay with it?"

"He has no say. You know your grandmother when she wants her own way."

"I do,' smiling. 'See you soon. Hopefully I can sneak away from Braun and Nana, and come see you on my terms."

"Good luck with that. Now off to bed you go."

"Love you lots."

"Right back at you baby girl."

Looking at Braun he said; "Nana got everything from the house. Plus she jammed their signal."

"I know. Hence they did not know that my mother was a hologram."

"No"

"Are they in New Earth?"

"Yes"

"Thank you."

"You are welcome."

Spending two years with Braun and his family, Free met someone. He was one of Braun's friends brother. He was cute Freedom thought, and she took an instant liking to him.

Seeing him every day, and with Braun stationed halfway around the globe, Freedom welcomed her new friend, and love interest in her life.

"Dr. Daniels, not now." Not wanting to talk to him.

"Now Freedom. The technology works. Do you know the medical implications of this? Delicate heart surgeries can be done by doctors now with this machine. Heart transplants will now be a thing of the past because, this machine can reverse heart attacks, and congestive heart failure. Pace Makers will become a thing of the past. Baby, you are more than a genius. You are a life saver."

"Yes, the new heart as you call it."

"It is a new heart for millions of people Freedom. We are the first and only company to design this machine. A machine that has and have tested to have a 100% success rate. People won't have to wait years for help anymore."

"I know, but I want something else."

"We did it baby," spinning Freedom around.

"We did. Listen I am going to head home. I am tired."

● ● ●

"Are you sure you're okay?" *worried concerned for Free.*

"I'm fine." Taking her home Nana was concerned because she usually wasn't tired.

"You are not fine. You like him, and you are tired from thinking about him, and wondering if he likes you in the same way." *Reading Freedom like a book.*

"Nana"

"I know you. You like him too much because I don't like him."

"Why? He's a nice guy. Besides, he's Braun's friend's brother?"

"For which I do not trust. He's not a young man with ethics. He's bad news, and you should not see him, or date him."

"Nana"

"You are eighteen years old tomorrow young lady."

"And I am hoping he will ask me out for my birthday, and you better not block his call."

"I will block his call because you are spending your eighteenth birthday with me, Braun's family, and some of his friends."

"Then I hope his brother take him to the house, so I can talk to him, and make you super jealous. I am hoping he will kiss me too."

"Yuk, he's not good enough for you. So no kissing the enemy."

"Nana have some fun. You know I should build you a Nano bot, and have him fall madly in love with you so that you can cut me some slack."

"I will not cut you any slack young lady."

"You will once I create this Nano bot for you."

"You will do no such thing. I am to protect you."

"You do, now, let me see the dress you have picked out for me for my eighteenth birthday."

"No, you will see it tomorrow."

"Please, pretty please Nana."

"No. Tomorrow you will see it, and Braun is calling you."

"Answer," and she saw Braun on the monitor.

"Hey gorgeous." *Said Braun and Freedom chuckled.*

"Hey beautiful."

● ● ●
46

"Looking forward to your eighteenth birthday tomorrow?"

"Yes"

"And she's also looking forward to seeing Craig, Duke's brother. She's smitten by him." Said Nana.

"Nana", scolded Freedom.

"Yes, Nana. Cut her some slack, because she's a woman now as she has been reminding me for the last couple of days."

"Braun", scolded Freedom.

"I know Nana has warned you about Craig, so truly be careful."

"I will be."

"Now, how did the preliminary tests go?"

"One hundred percent success rate."

"Have we done any human trials?"

"They were humans trials."

"What?" Surprised that the tests were a success, but then; he knew better because she was driven with more than true passion when it came to saving lives. She was a true human being, inventor, and creator. life, and preserving life...was her goal, and true passion". He knew that first hand.

47

"I do truly love what I do you know."

"I know, and I trust you wholeheartedly, you know."

"I know." *you do, so no worries.*

"So my beauty. What does she want for her eighteenth birthday?"

"You to be there for me, but I know you can't get away. Am, but I will see him soon," holding back the tears. She had so wanted to celebrate her eighteenth birthday with him.

"Come on let me see those dreamy eyes of yours." *Smiling at her because he heard the hurt — her voice as well as saw the disappointment on her face.*

"No, they are too gorgeous for you."

"You think so."

"I know so, besides, these eyes are only for Craig." And he burst out laughing because he knew she was holding back tears.

"Hey, you will always be my true sunshine."

"I'd better be. See you later beautiful."

"I will be thinking of you."

"You'd better be." And he was gone. Wiping his face he looked at her picture as he held her protectively.

Going to bed; later Nana called Braun.

• • •

"You have to be there for her you know. I think Craig is just a front for the way she truly feels about you."

"Nana she's but a child."

"A child that you've grown to have feelings for. A child that is now a woman that you've protected with your life. You've put up so many defences to protect her, and have protected her. She trusts you wholeheartedly Braun. I know she was holding back tears of not having you at her eighteenth birthday."

"I am too old for her Nana."

"Are you, or are you just masking your true love for her."

"Yeah" *he had come to rely on Freedom for so much.*
"Be there for her like she has been there for you."

"Yes mam." *He still did not knw what to do.*

Driving Freedom to Braun's parents home; Freedom was wide eyed at the amount of people that was there. People she had not seen in a while was there including her parents and siblings.

"Mom"

"We can only stay for a couple of minutes. The air here is not pure therefore, we cannot last in this environment for too long."

"I thought that was fixed."

"It's not, nor do people want to come back here. The environment we are in is too peaceful and pure. Our world is stable." Baby we are in paradise, and life is truly calm and beautiful."

"Mom"

"Happy eighteenth birthday baby." enjoy yourself, and enjoy life."

All the important people she needed was there for a few minutes; then they had to leave.

"See you soon, but we have to go," and they were gone.

"Mom, everyone."

"Baby it's okay."

"I don't want them to leave Nana."

"They have to baby."

"I want to go with them," crying.

"Things are not fully stabilized there. You have to give them more time. Please hang in there."

"Yeah." hurt that her family and friends could not stay longer.

"Hey, dry your tears. I am here with you, and you will be fine."

"Yeah," and she walked away from Nana.

Feeling her pain, Nana caught up to her and held her from behind. Dancing with her as if it was Braun dancing with her Nana sang her; *No Woman Nuh Cry by Bob Marley* perfectly in his voice. Relaxing as she thought of Braun, she let the music, and Nana's movement soothe her, and she dried her tears, and relaxed in Nana's arms.

"Thank you, I needed that."

"She is welcome. Now guests are beginning to arrive, so chin up and relax. And no thinking about Craig. He is a wayward boy that will influence you negatively with his charm."

"Nana"

"Stay grounded and focused. I know you are not experienced in boys, and emotions."

"Am too, you taught me."

"Yes I did, but with all I have taught you, human emotions are not the same as robot emotions. Yes, I can feel, but it is not the same. I am programmed to feel."

"Did you want me to take away your programming?"

"And lose my best friend; no. I am sworn to protect you, and I will protect you at all cost. Trust him not because he is not who he seem. He is wayward."

"Thank you mom."

"Anytime my child. Come, let me help you to get dressed."

"Are you going to let me wear makeup?"

"Do you want to wear makeup?"

"No. I just want to be me, but a grown up me; well a eighteen-year-old me."

"Braun are you okay?" Nana asked when Freedom was in the shower.

"I will be."

"She stole the prototype?" Nana asked

"She unveiled it."

"But you knew she would do this. Freedom was her game, and financial gain."

"I tried so much to prevent this. I even took her off the project you know, only to have her do this to me."

"Should I tell Freedom?"

"No, I will tell her when I see her. For now let her enjoy her day."

"Braun, she does care about you."

● ● ●

"I know, and I know she will be devasted, but what can I do? She worked so hard for this; to have them take her glory yet again."

"Could you not do something?"

"No, take care of her for me."

"Braun trust her. Do not do anything stupid. You know Free, she always has a backup plan."

"This was her invention. He could not move forward because he did not know what to do. She made his idea into a reality now for her, and him to shatter her like this; I cannot allow."

"And I said to trust Free. Do not do anything that will hurt her and you. Trust is all you need Braun, and you know this. I trust Free at all cost, you should do the same."

"Yes"

"I mean it, now I have to go. You be good." And Nana was gone.

"Nana is everything alright?" Free asked as she came out of the shower.

"Everything is fine, now sit while I do up your hair."

"You're not going to be rough are you?"

"I have learnt to be gentler when it comes to combing, and styling your natural hair." And she sat down, and Nana played *Just To Be Close To You by The Commodores* while she styled Freedom's hair.

"You will always be close to me, never you forget that do you hear me," said Nana.

"I know, and I will never forget."

Styling and dressing Freedom in the most beautiful blue gown she had ever seen, she had looked more beautiful than a story book princess. She was gorgeous, and when Braun's dad came to get her to bring her downstairs; his mouth dropped to how gorgeous and beautiful she looked.

Walking down the stairs with her, everyone just stared at them in amazement. Seeing the beauty in front of him, Craig could not help himself. All he kept saying was wow. He was seeing Free's true beauty for the first time, and he loved what he saw. Freedom was jaw dropping gorgeous all done up.

With Craig monopolizing her all night, she did not get to dance with anyone but him. She had no time to breathe, and Free did not like that.

"You know you can share me with everyone."

"Nope, can't share you. You are mine all evening." And she was his all evening. Glad for the night to be ended she thanked Braun's family for making her eighteenth birthday a complete success as well as, told them she

● ● ●

was sorry for the way in which Craig monopolized her all evening.

"Are you going home tonight?" Asked Braun's mother.

"Yes, Nana has a gift for me at home."

"I am sorry that Braun could not be here."

"That's okay. I am sure Nana sent him pictures of me in my dress all done up; especially his father walking me down the stairs."

"You deserve all the happiness in the world. You are not only smart but true."

"My different mother's raised me right. Made sure that I grew with values; good values, and good ethics."

"Happy birthday Free," said all.

"Thank you," and Freedom was gone with Nana.

Going home Nana gave her her gift. A beautiful diamond bracelet.

"I made it you know."

"I know you did, but where did you find these diamonds?"

"There is more to home than you think."

"Thank you."

"You are welcome. Now I have a special surprise for you."

"Nana, this is more than enough. I could not ask for more."

"No." Hearing Braun's voice she turned and darted in his arms. Looking in his eyes she kissed him real hard. That was the first time she was kissing someone. Realizing what she was doing she pulled away from him and said, "I am so sorry. I should not have done that."

Touching her face warmly he said, "please don't be. I've wanted to do that for the longest while, but you were not of age, and now that you are, I have no regrets in you kissing me."

"Are you sure?"

"Quite," and he pulled her into his arms and kissed her. Clearing her throat both realized that Nana was still in the room.

"Mom I am so sorry."

"Do not be. You are with the right person never you forget that. Like you, I trust him wholeheartedly with you."

"Nana"

"You are both safe. Now talk, and talk as it's her birthday." And Nana was gone.

• • •

"What does she mean by those words Braun?"

"It's your birthday, and I don't want to spoil it. Now come and open your gift from me because I know you are expecting one from me."

"I have my present already; you."

"You are truly beautiful you know that."

"Thank you."

"I did not want you talking to him you know."

"I got that feeling. Plus, I know your body language, but I do not know how you feel, this is why I wanted, and needed to pursue this."

"Even with knowing that he was not honest."

"I'm sorry Braun, but I couldn't tell you how I felt about you. I was so young. Now that I am eighteen, I can tell you because I hide nothing from you. I did fall in love with you truthfully. As I got to know you, I wanted to tell you, and tell you I wanted to pursue a relationship with you, but couldn't. I know you protected me at all cost. I know you kept all undesirables from me including the intellectual ones."

"It was hard for me you know."

"I know, and I know that's why you left to take up residence in the next office."

"I truly love you you know."

"Then stay in my life and not leave. Call me stupid, but I truly love when you are around me. Just like Nana, I don't want her to leave. I cherish her a great deal, and I do listen to her."

"Then marry me. Be my wife." He could not let her go. She was of legal age. He had to have her in his life. *She was his world and things. He could not let anyone else have he*

"Are you sure, because I've never been with a man before?"

"I know all about you remember. And yes, I am sure. I need you to be my wife." *I need you in my life.*

"Then yes."

"Good girl." And he once again kissed her.

Hearing the sirens go off, Freedom ran to her room, and almost collided with Nana as she went to retrieve her laptop.

"There is more and more instability and seismic activity," said Freedom.

"Are the tectonic plates becoming more and more unstable?" Asked Braun

"Yes," said Freedom.

"Can we get a secure line to the others?"

"There are no secure lines for connection."

"What does that mean?"

"We have to wait a couple of days."

"Nana"

"You have to bring your family here Braun." *Said nana. She was was concerned for their safety.*

"Free" *needing reassurance from her.*

"It's safer. Remember your parents home is on a major Faultline."

Scrambling to the phone Braun called his parents. He could not use his regular home phone, or cellular device. He had a secure line, and phone that Freedom set up for him and his family. In all Freedom did, she secured their future. She knew they were watched; monitored, and she had to keep many steps ahead of them all. *She had built an impenetrable fortress for Braun and his family.*

Her advancements, science, medicine; technology wise they wanted, but she refused to let any government gain access to her creations, modifications, knowledge, and more. She walked free; feared them not because her security forces they knew nothing about, nor could they infiltrate. *She was smarter than them therefore, she was way ahead of them.*

"Mom are you, dad, and sis okay?" He hurriedly asked before his mom could say hello.

"We are fine, we just had a minor tremor that's all."

• • •

"I'll be right there."

"Braun"

"Mom, I will be right there. Nana get the chopper ready. Mom get all your personal belongings; and be ready."

"Yes sir."

"I will stay here and monitor the situation," said Freedom.

"I am not leaving you gorgeous, so let's go. You can monitor everything from the chopper."

Scrambling to get to the chopper; within fifteen minutes Nana was landing at Braun's parents home.

Rushing to the house Braun said; "Mom, dad, sis let's go."

"Braun we are safe here." said his mother.

"You are not safe here mom, now let's go before the earth crumbles beneath our feet."

"It was a minor tremor Braun."

"I know mom, but this minor tremor is a catalyst for a major one, and you know this. So let's go."

"Son"

Seeing Freedom rushing to them she said; "mom we have to go, you have less than fifteen minutes to get your things before a sinkhole devours us."

"Sweetheart please let's go. This is just a house. A house I know you do not want to leave, but we have to. All of our essentials are at Braun's home, please just let this place go."

Feeling the earth quake beneath them; Braun's mother screamed.

"Please mom, we have to go." Scrambling to get to the chopper Nana lift off in no time. Looking back from a distance Braun's mother saw her home being devoured in a sink hole. Nothing was left of the house, and Free held her.

"I am so sorry for your loss."

"I know."

Going to his home, Braun held his mother tight. She could not comprehend what was happening, but she knew things were for the best. Things were getting worse and worse each day. The lack of food, polluted drinking water, severe global shortage of medicine, lack of farm land, diseases, looting, killings. Earth had become the haven for all that is wicked and evil. People didn't care about saving themselves, or having a better environment on earth. Hate was still in the hearts of (the) many. No one took the time to think or, come up with solutions to save the planet truthfully. And with

• • •

Earth crumbling, no one in power knew what to do. They could not save Earth.

Earth was literally crumbling around them. Sink holes could not be repaired hence, the many caves; caverns globally. In many lands; you could not walk, or go anywhere due to the hearts of men; people that had no cause to live. Therefore, violent crimes of theft, rape, and murder was nothing new in many lands. This was the norm. No one was safe because it was survival of the fittest; not just for the poor, but for those in high society; the elite few. Even in their society; the society of the elite few; strife reigned. They too were facing shortage of food, and improper drinking water.

Money; their wealth and money meant nothing anymore because, money had no use; could not buy the necessities they needed to sustain and maintain them. Life was dismal for (the) many, but gorgeous for the chosen few; those who had the sense, and common sense to secure their future. Their future was intact; safe thus; New Earth was up and running.

In Earth; Lies were told, and people lived by the lies they were told. taught.

No one saw that they were conditioned to believe the lies, and deceit of them who ran the globe due to religion, politics, economics, and science. greed.

"Everything is going to be okay, you will see." trying to reassure of his mother of everything.

"Braun, the world is becoming more and more unstable. More disasters, less food, more sinkholes that cannot be repaired. With all your inventions, could you not do something?"

"We did do something mom."

"What?"

"Please trust me."

"I do."

"Then no worries." *you are safe, and you will have a better life."*

Going into work the following Monday, Braun told Freedom what happened. *He did not want to, but he had to. He could not hide this from her.*

~~I will am~~ sorry they stole your idea Free. I wanted to protect your invention, but while they were helping you to make your prototype, they were creating one of their own."

"Please don't be sorry. They did not win, because their device will never work. I told you, I did not trust them; therefore, Nana and I came up with fake designs." *Designs they unveiled without doing any trials on their prototype.*

"But you said the tests were successful."

"Yes, holograms cannot lie once you've designed it to give off certain effects."

"Freedom"

"I do not like to be used, nor do I like governments. Therefore, I refuse to help them. They helped to create this mess on land, but no one want to help clean the mess; not that it can be cleaned. And I refuse to help them. I will not clean their mess up for them." And she did not. In all the governments of the globe did; they lied and deceived; caused billions to lose their life. Many did listen to their leaders, and earth was in total disarray. *No one saw the ramifications of their sins, actions, more population, less land space, less food to eat, polluted waters; the total decay of all life.*

"Nana"

"The first and second beacon has been sent."

"It's early," *said Braun*

"They did say it might be," *replied Nana.*

Waiting for a couple of days, the families of staff was safely home.

"What will happen to the rest of the population up here?" *asked Braun's mother.*

"I truly do not know," said Free. *The left behinds were not her concern, the people of New Earth was/were.*

"You cannot just leave them to die." Supplied Braun's mother. *She was horrified, she needed to know that the people were going to be okay.*

"Baby, when we offered so many of our friends an opportunity to join us on this project; they laughed in our face saying this could not be done. When I presented what I wanted to do to the public, they too laughed at me, and said I should be committed. I was a fraud. I lost funding, virtually all of my friends. Those I knew in high places denied knowing me, nor did they

• • •

under creation
any creation
or circumstances

want to associate with me, and my family. Many of my family members, and yours turned against us, wanted nothing to do with us. So I cannot save them, and I would hope you feel the same way. I cannot have compassion for them, because they did all to hurt us physically. They did all to tear our family a part, and I refuse to forgive them, or save them. They contributed nothing to our efforts, and now that New Earth is up and running, I will not save them," Braun's father said. He had endured a lot of ridicule, and pain. He could not endure anymore, nor could he save people that did not want to be saved. *He did try, and was refused.*

"Mom remember you pleaded with some of the wives you knew that was *were* married to politicians, and none came on board with you. You were the muse for them, so truly let them be. They did not want good for self. You also gave the global population a chance to come on board, and we were rejected. In all New Earth has, we only have over a million people. Over a million people that sacrificed their life, and life's earnings here for a better place to live war free, violence free, religion free, hate free, political free, and they have it," Braun reminded his mother. *He knew the pain and hurt his parents felt. He saw their fears as well. Now they had a better way and he*

"But we do not know how long we can live there *was not long* Braun." *to let them*

that did
"Mom, New Earth is going, and there are people there *not want*
that are over one hundred and fifty years old that is *better for self*
healthy, looks great, and feel great. You cannot tell they *have a way*
are over one hundred and fifty years old to how young *to new*
and ageless they look. Trust me, they all look better *into Earth.*

than a thirty year old on this level; up here in upper earth, so no worries. It's time to live so live."

"I'm sorry son, but I just wanted more people to come with us, but like you always say, people will forever make bad choices for self and or, wait until the last minute when things are too late to save self."

"We can't wait until the last minute mom," said Free.

"Everything is aligned. We need to send the last beacon," said the commander from New Earth.

"Not all will be ready."

"All is ready, send up the shuttle for the rest of the people. Many are enroute, and many will need a couple of days. We cannot delay with this time line. Upper Earth is crumbling more and more. We cannot wait until Marshall Law come into effect. We need to get our people out of there now," said the Commander.

"There is about one hundred thousand that is still not accounted for."

"You have no confirmation from them."

"No"

Calling Nana, the commander said; "Nana, there is about one hundred thousand people that have not been accounted for, are there any interference? If there are, secure a signal, and send out the different signals. You and the others know what to do, let's get this done."

"Yes sir."

"It's coffee time," was sent out by Nana and the others, and within two days all was accounted for, and headed to their pick-up destination.

While the world was in turmoil; those that had a new home was being safely transported to New Earth. No one was the wiser. That was the way they needed things to be done, and it was done. None was missed because they way they left was as if they were going on vacation to another land. All had their ticket; travel documents in order, so little by little they left for New Earth.

"Mom, you, dad, and sis have to go."

"I'm not leaving you."

"You have to go mom. I need you to be safe."

"I need you to be safe also."

"I will be; now go. I will see you soon."

"Braun"

"Mom, I need everything to be secured here before I can join you. Please for your safety, trust me and go," and she was gone leaving Freedom, Braun, and Nana behind.

"All has been accounted for, please come home," they received two weeks later.

Hey gorgeous, I'm outside your office building, but it seems as if no one is here."

"All the staff has gone home, and I am on my way out."

"I want to take you out for lunch."

"I'm sorry but I can't go to lunch with you, please understand."

"I do, but tell Mr. Boss Man I say, he works you too hard."

"I will."

"Free, we have to go now." And she felt the building shake. Seeing Craig scramble to get to his jeep as he sped away Free, Braun, and Nana scurried to get to safety. Securely tucked away in their shuttle Free huddled to Nana and Braun. Nothing for them was left behind apart from structure; houses, and empty offices; buildings. All Freedom's inventions were safely in New Earth. She made sure no one in Old Earth could recreate her work. She was determined not to help the left behinds, and she did. Did not help them, or leave anything behind to help them now, and in the future.

Reaching safety after a week, they were with family and friends. Happy to be home to a beautiful world, and a new beginning, Free sat with Braun by the seashore. They had left the turmoil of old earth behind.

• • •

They had a new start now hence; this was their true and new beginning thanks to Freedom, and all involved in this new creation – New Earth.

"It's beautiful," said Braun. He was seeing the greenery, abundance of trees. Trees that had fruits; lots of fruits on them. There was no smog, just clear blue skies without any white clouds. *Just a perfect light blue sky with meaning.*

"I'm glad you like it."

"I do. This earth is as beautiful as you."

"Thank you."

"I never doubted you, you know. I trusted you from day one. You were so young, but I trusted you anyway."

'I know."

"Why did you save me though?"

"I found him special, and I knew I could save him."

"The doctors gave me no chance to live."

"Ah, what do they know? They are just text book junkies that do not know how the body fully works."

"Energy and or, kinetic flow; vibration amongst other things?" Braun asked

"Yes"

"Was I the first one you saved with your machine?"

"Yes"

"Thank you for saving me."

"Anytime."

"There you two are," said Nana.

"Are we needed?" Asked Freedom

"No, I was just lonely that's all."

"Nana, what did you do to Nano Bot?" asked free

"I turned him off."

"Why?"

"I needed time with the both of you."

"You know Nano Bot can turn himself on."

"I know, and he knows the rules. I have to protect the both of you."

"Thanks mom," resting her head on Nana.

"You are welcome."

"They are fine. We are safe," said Freedom's mother to Nano Bot.

• • •

"I know we are, but they are so close."

"They will always be close. Nana is her true best friend."

"So am I."

"She knows. They will have children soon, and you will be more than busy."

"Babies," said Nano Bot.

"Yes babies."

"Should I be preparing now?"

"Nana will tell you."

"I will be a father, just like Nana is a mother."

"Yes, therefore Free is truly free."

"Thank you for your trust," said Nana.

"You are most welcome," said Freedom.

"Come, it's going to rain."

Going home Free stood inside watching the rain as Braun held her from behind.

"Everything is in balance?"

"Yes, but you are worried?"

"Children?"

"There are plenty of children here."

"The atmosphere has changed Free."

"I know, but it does not mean we can't have children. We can. We are pure beings now, and our energy fields have changed. The new comers like us have to be educated all over again. We are not dependant on blood to govern our body, but water to cleanse and purify our body and spirit; energy."

"Is that why there is so much water?"

"Yes. Two different water system that expand as the population expands; grow."

"And above?"

"As the earth above crumble and sink, *New Earth takes the place of the old one.*"

"That sun and moon?"

"Will become our secondary fuel source. A new solar system is being formed, stars that we can see. A secondary sun and moon that we can see. All that was, and that will be left of that earth is the sun and moon. The sun and moon is our reminder of the left behinds, those that did not want to be saved. This is our new beginning Braun, a new beginning of truth, where there is no need to have armies, greed, fighting; all that was.

● ● ●

We have a new and clean slate. We are free to live free."

"You know I thought about how our children will be."

"They will be fine. In this world, as the population increase so does the land space. That was the hard part, but we found the solution."

"Why not create a earth within earth like you did here?"

"There is no need for that. Because we have a secondary sun and moon, a baby planet is being formed. A habitable planet that is accessible to all. Think of it as a vacation home away from home. Besides, all the evils; sins of Old Earth we did not want here. We needed a clean place and slate, and we have that here."

"But why not try to clean up Old Earth?"

"For whom Braun? Man; humans created so much mess. Those that wanted and needed a better way have it – New Earth. I, nor anyone should have to clean up the mess of those who truly do not care; only to have them mess it all up again. Earth could not take anymore abuse and pain Braun. She was severely suffering. She had to die; give up her ghost to be reborn again. This planet is New Earth Braun; our good and true land. So be truly happy. No worries."

"I have none now because you are not only my Freedom, but you are my tomorrow as well."

● ● ●

"I'm glad because I want, and need my children with you."

"Will it not be painful?" And she pinched him.

"I did not feel that."

"Then you know, all pain is taken away. Baby enjoy life because life; good and true life is there to enjoy."

"Prove it." And she turned and kissed him, and Nana smiled.

The End – well a new beginning. There is no end to truth.

and at that moment Nana played One Love by Bob Marley. There was no place — on Earth for the hopeless sinner who have hurt all Mankind. NO politicans, no religous leaders, no religous fanatics, no racist religion of anykind allowed — New Earth. This was a new beginning for those who truly wanted a better way of life. They who wanted and needed to be saved from it all, the choas, confusion, war, violence, death, hatred, and lies of Upper Earth. Browns money and power did play with Mankind, and they were categorically rejected by Mankind. New Earth could not save the hopeless sinners. those That rejected a saving grace was left to cry and die because they did not want better.

good for self and family,
including others. Their
saviour did come = the
form of a female black
child.